*to Dewayne
From
Uncle George*

LUKE

BY

GEORGE E DAVISON

*Enjoy
GEDavison*

Luke

All Rights Reserved © 2013 by
George Davison

No part of this book may be reproduced or transmitted in any form or by any means, graphic, electronic, or mechanical, including photocopying, recording, taping, or by any information storage retrieval system, without the written permission of the publisher.

Printed in the United States of America
By www.lulu.com

Cover photo by Karla Davison Brown
Of author's father, Oscar Davison

TABLE OF CONTENTS

FOREWORD 4

CHAPTER ONE: The Fall Roundup 8

CHAPTER TWO: Crown King 13

CHAPTER THREE: Prescott 22

CHAPTER FOUR: Winter at the Ranch 33

CHAPTER FIVE: Springtime in the Mountains
....42

CHAPTER SIX: Summer at the Ranch...........49

About the Author..65

Cover photo is author's father Oscar Davison
Photo by Karla Davison Brown

FOREWORD

I want to thank my friend Pat who after reading one of my short stories, suggested that I should write more about the man named Luke. I started out writing another short story, then another one and then I put them all together and came up with this book. Thank you Pat for the inspiration.

When I was a little boy growing up on the farm, I wanted to be a cowboy. It seemed like such a glamorous life, riding around on horseback all day, playing the guitar, and singing songs to the ladies and shooting the bad guys. I wanted to be just like Gene Autry and Roy Rogers. As I got older I came to realize that a cowboys' life wasn't that glamorous, it was a lot of hard work. This book is what I would imagine it would really be like to be a cowboy, living alone on a remote ranch in the mountains of Arizona. It is not a true story and should not be taken as such. It is jut how I feel, now that I am older but maybe not wiser, about what the life of a cowboy would really be like. It is not so glamorous.

While doing some checking for this book I came across some information that surprised me. While Gene Autry and Roy Rogers made it appear that the guitar was the musical instrument of choice for most cowboys some claim that the banjo was much more popular than the guitar. The banjo is smaller and much easier to pack and carry around than the guitar.

Another popular instrument was the concertina, a smaller version of the accordion. Then there was the harmonica or mouth organ as we use to call it and the Jews' harp, a small musical instrument that is held between the teeth. It has a thin flexible metal strip that gives off a twanging sound when struck with the fingers. Both of these instruments were small enough to fit easily into a saddle bag or could even be carried in your pocket. Did you ever see a cowboy riding around with a set of drums tied to the back of his horse? Of course not. Their choice for a percussion instrument was to beat on the bottom of their tin coffee cups with a spoon. Or they would play percussion with the claves or the maracas or the bones. Now you have probably never heard of the bones but that is just what they were: bones. They were the rib bones taken from a cow scrapped clean, polished and cut in about six inch length. You took two in each hand and held them between your fingers and beat a rhythm with them by striking them together as you moved you wrist up and down. My grandpa use to play the bones. His were made of highly polished wood and would give off a clickety clack sound when they were struck together. One day when I was a kid I got grandpa's bones and was fooling around with them trying to figure out how to play them. When grandpa caught me he played percussion on the seat of my pants. You didn't fool around with grandpa's bones.

As I said there may not be much truth in this book and one of the reasons for that may be because I use to hunt and camp in the area where this story takes place and I would get my drinking water from the Hassayampa River. I found out later that the natives all say that if you drink water from the Hassayampa River you will never tell the truth again.

So enjoy.

THE BRADSHAW MOUNTAINS

Some times it appeared that he was all alone
As he rode around the mountains that he called home
Just a man and his horse riding around
A long way from the nearest town

The Bradshaw Mountains he called home
But he was never really all alone
For he always had his trusted horse
That he could always talk to of course

There was a bald eagle circling in the sky
As a covey of quails scurried for cover near by
A big old coyote would cross his trail
Moving fast like he was carrying the mail

A group of jackrabbits would just set there and stare
As long as he didn't get too close they didn't seem to care
And when the buzzard started circling in the sky
It could mean there was a dead carcass near by

A herd of javelina running for cover
They looked like they would run into each other
A herd of mule deer feeding on the ridge
He could cross the Hassayampa River without a bridge

There was life abundant all around
There was no need to live in town
For he was never all alone
In the Bradshaw Mountains he called home

CHAPTER ONE: The Fall Roundup

The sun was just going down behind the mountain ridges to the west, casting long shadows across the valley floor as Luke drove the small herd of cattle across the Hassayampa River and into the holding corral at the River Pasture. It had been a good two day roundup and he had been able to find his prize bull and most of his breeding stock. Without good breeding stock you couldn't build up and maintain your herd size. Luke was a small rancher compared to most of the ranchers around him and new to the area. He ran a one man operation, doing most of the work himself, occasionally taking on a drifter to give him a hand when the work load got heavy.

Luke had started out with a small ranch in Kansas but had been slowly crowded out by the bigger ranchers. Then when the sod busters came in and started plowing up the good grazing land he decided to sell out and head west. He settled in on the western slopes of the Bradshaw Mountains, south of Prescott in the heart of the Arizona Territory. The land was much more rugged that it had been in Kansas and it took more land to sustain the same number of cattle. But he shouldn't have to worry about farmers coming in and trying to farm the area. He had been there three years now and had his herd built up to a manageable size, just about right for a one man operation.

Luke swung the corral gate closed behind the last steer and sat there on his horse for a few minutes trying to get a count on the cattle in the corral. It looked like he may be missing a few steers maybe a half dozen. Luke unsaddled his horse and gave him a good rubdown before hobbling him and turning him loose to graze with the pack mule. He wouldn't go far and Luke wouldn't have any trouble catching him in the morning.

Luke built a small fire and started fixing supper. He skinned the rabbit he had shot earlier today and hung it over the fire to roast. He would have fresh meat tonight instead of cold beef jerky. He had seen a herd of javelina this afternoon but they were too far away to shoot.

He would like to be able to get one of them to give him something besides beef to eat once in a while. The javelina were good eating you just had to be careful when you skinned them and make sure you didn't break or touch their musk sac or you would spoil the meat. Maybe he would be lucky and get close enough to get a shot at them tomorrow. Or maybe he could kill a mule deer: he had seen a lot of tracks the last two days, and knew there were a lot of deer in the area. That would be a real treat. He had seen a couple of nice mule deer bucks in the area earlier in the summer but didn't want to shoot them then because it was too warm and the meat wouldn't keep. The weather was cold enough now, in late October that the meat would keep and wouldn't spoil on him.

Luke finished eating his supper and washed the dishes and put them away. Then he rolled himself a cigarette, lighting it with a burning stick from the fire and poured himself another cup of coffee. Sitting down on his bed roll with his back resting against the corral fence he contemplated his plans for the next few days. Tomorrow he would ride up to the top of Fire Clay Hill and work his way back down, checking out the side canyons on the way. Hopefully he would be able to find the rest of his missing stock. Then the following day he would drive the herd back down to the main ranch. Once he got the herd home and settled in the winter pasture he would cut out about a dozen of the older and prime steers and drive them over to the mining camp at Crown King. He could get a better price for his steers by selling them directly to the miners than he could by selling them to the cattle buyers in Prescott. That would work out better for both him and the miners. By cutting out the middle man, the cattle buyers, they would both come out ahead.

After he got back from Crown King he would take a day off to rest up, then he would hook up the wagon and head into Prescott to load up on supplies for the winter. He wanted to make the trip to Prescott before the snow came. They didn't get a lot of snow in the area but it was no fun getting caught in one of the sudden snow storms that could pop up, so he had better make the trip early. He needed some barbwire for fencing and some blocks of salt for the cattle. He wanted to have enough flour, coffee, sugar, oatmeal and tobacco on hand to see him through the winter. He didn't want to have to make another trip into Prescott until spring. Once he got to Prescott he would spend the evening on Whisky Row and probably spend the night with one of the ladies in her boudoir, before heading home the following day. It would be a good trip.

The moon had just started to come up over the ridges to the east and there wasn't a cloud in the sky. It was going to get cold tonight. Clear and cold that is the way it would be for the next couple of nights. Occasionally a coyote would let out a howl and Luke could hear the yapping of a pack of coyote pups in their den over under the edge of the cliff on the south end of the canyon. They wouldn't bother him and he was used to their singing, it might make the horse and mule a little edgy but they would be all right.

Luke unrolled his bed roll and got ready to settle down for a night's sleep. Before crawling into his bed roll he got his rope and strung it around his bed roll. He didn't want to wake up in the morning and find a rattlesnake in bed with him. Someone had told him once that those rattlesnakes will not craw across a rope and that would keep them out. He didn't know if it was true or not. Maybe it was just a myth but he wasn't going to take any chances. He strung his rope around his bed roll every time he had to sleep out on the ground and so far he had never woken up with a rattlesnake in bed with him. Maybe it worked and maybe it didn't but it seemed to work for him. Just one more night of sleeping out on the ground after tonight, then he would be back in his own bed at the ranch house. The fall roundup would be over.

CHAPTER TWO: Crown King

Luke got up early in the morning, the fall roundup had been over for three days now and he had been able to spend the last three nights sleeping in his own bed in the ranch house instead of rolling up in the blankets on the ground under the stars. But it was time to hit the trail again. He had spent the last three day checking the fence around the winter pasture and making sure the herd was getting settled down in their new surroundings. Yesterday he had cut out the steers he wanted to sell, separating them from the rest of the herd, and putting them in a small holding corral near the barn.

He finished his breakfast of pancakes, eggs and bacon, and downed a cup of hot coffee. It could be his last hot meal for a couple of days, he would have to get by on sandwiches and jerky until he got the steers delivered to the mining camp at Crown King. He made some sandwiches and put them in a small pack along with some jerky, can peaches and some can beans. Then he headed for the barn. He threw his camping pack on the pack mule along with his small pack of food; he would have to spend at least one night camping out before he got to Crown King. He secured the packs on the mule and then saddled his horse and led them both out of the barn.

The sun was just coming up over the Bradshaw Mountains to the east when he got to the corral. He swung the gate open before he climbed into the saddle and rode into the corral. Luke circled around behind the steers prodding a couple of them that were still lying down to their feet. "Come on doggies, let's get moving" he said as he slapped them on the rear with his rope. "Where are we going now?" they seem to ask as Luke herded them out of the corral and started them moving east. "None of your business," Luke told them, "Just get moving." He didn't want to tell them that they were going to slaughter. He had a little trouble getting them started. They wanted to go back to the pasture where the rest of the herd was and he had to keep heading them off and turning them around to get them headed in the direction he wanted them to go. "Come on us cattle have feeling too, you know?" They seem to say. "We want to stay here with the rest of our family and friends." Once they were out of sight of the pasture and the rest of the herd, they settled down and moved along without too much prodding.

They crossed the Hassayampa River and moved east into the higher regions of the Bradshaw Mountains. The low laying sage brush slowly gave way to scattering stands of pine trees. The further east they went, the higher up in the mountains they got, the thicker the pine trees were. The rest of the day went by pretty uneventfully, the steers moved along at a leisurely pace, once in a while one would start to wander off the trail and Luke would have to head him off and get him back on track but most of the time there was no problem and Luke just had to follow along behind. It was getting late in the afternoon and they had passed the half way point when they arrived at a place called Box Canyon. It was a small box canyon just off the main trail and had a small spring just inside the entrance to the canyon. Luke turned the small herd into the canyon; it would be a good place to spend the night. There was fresh water and foliage for them to feed on and he wouldn't have to worry about them wandering off in the night.

Luke made his camp right at the mouth of the canyon, the entrance was narrow and there was no way any of the steers could get out without him knowing it. He unpacked the pack mule and turned him lose in the canyon then he unsaddled his horse and gave him a good rubdown and some oats before he hobbled him and turned him loose.

Luke built a small campfire and made a pot of coffee and opened a can of beans to go with his sandwich for supper. At least the coffee and beans would help warm him up a little bit. It was already getting cold out and the sun wouldn't set for another hour yet. It was going to be a cold one tonight. Luke didn't get much sleep that night, it was too cold and he had to keep the fire going all night long. He would sleep for awhile then the cold would wake him up and he would get up and put some more wood on the fire then go back to sleep until the cold would wake him up again. He was up at the crack of dawn and made a fresh pot of coffee to warm him up and get him started again. After a couple of cups of coffee and another cold sandwich he put the campfire out and then squatted down behind a bush to relieve himself before he went to catch his saddle horse and pack mule.

The saddle horse was no problem, he was feeding just inside the canyon and Luke was able to walk right up to him and put a halter on him. The pack mule was in an ornery mood this morning and every time Luke got close to him he would kick up his heels and run away. He should have hobbled him before he turned him loose last night. Luke was going to have to chase him down with the saddle horse this morning. Luke led the saddle horse back to camp and got him saddled then he went after the pack mule. The pack mule led him on a merry chase around the small canyon before he finely got a rope on him and led him back to the camp site. The steers seem to enjoy the show and just stood around chewing their cuds. Luke got the pack mule settled down and got the pack loaded on him then he went in after the steers and got them out of the canyon and back on the trail again.

They were high in the Bradshaw Mountains surrounded by Ponderosa pines by the time the sun came up in front of them. Things were looking good and moving along at a good pace. Baring any unforeseen misfortune Luke figured they should be in Crown King by late afternoon. About mid morning they came to a small stream and Luke let them stop for a drink and a short rest before pushing on. As he sat there on his horse looking around waiting for the steers to drink their full he thought he saw a movement in the brush off to one side. He gazed at the spot until it came into full focus; yes it was a mountain lion. Then it turned and disappeared into the surrounding brush. Luke wondered if the mountain lion had been following them for a while hoping to catch one of the steers off by himself away from the rest of the herd or had he by chance just happen to stop by for a drink at the stream and got scared away when they rode up. Luke didn't think he would try to take down one of the steers when they were all grouped together but if one got off by itself he would go after it. Anyway he had better keep his eyes open for the rest of the trip and not let his guard down. If anything happened to spook the steers and they took off running in this thick pine forest it could take him days to round them all up and he would probably never find all of them.

The rest of the day passed without any problems and it was late afternoon when they rode into Crown King and Luke herded the small herd into the empty corral behind the mine commissary and office then he went into the office to see what kind of deal he could work out. After the mine owner checked out the herd he and Luke sat down and they started haggling over the price for the herd. The mine owner had a slight advantage since he knew that Luke didn't want to take the herd home with him and there was no one else in town that could afford to buy them. But Luke knew what it would cost them if they had to go to Prescott to buy their beef. Luke drove a hard bargain and after a brief period of time they finally agreed on a price. It wasn't as much as Luke had hoped for but it was more that the buyers in Prescott were paying so he was satisfied. Luke took a small cash advance so he would have some money to spend while he was in town and received a bank draft for the balance. He would have to take the bank draft to Prescott to cash it.

Luke took his horse and the pack mule over to the livery stable and got them settled for the night. Then he headed over to the hotel and restaurant to get a hot meal and see what accommodations he could arrange for himself. After a leisurely supper he moseyed over to the saloon for a drink. After the last two days on the trail he figured he deserved a good stiff drink or two. Some of the miners were just getting a game of poker started and wanted to know if he wanted in on the action. They wanted some of his money. Luke decided to join them for a few hands but he wanted to be careful and make sure he didn't lose too much of his hard earned cash. After about an hour he folded his hand and cashed in his chips and left. Luck had been with him, he wasn't a big winner but he won a few dollars and didn't lose any of his hard earned cash before he quit.

Luke went back to the hotel and spent some time with Big Bertha, a huge big bosom motherly type woman who had come to Crown

King in answer to an ad for someone to come and minister to the needs of the love starved miners. She was good at her job and knew how to satisfy a man's cravings. Then he went back to his own room and turned in for the night.

Luke was up early the next morning and had a big breakfast at the hotel's restaurant then he went over to the livery stable to get his horse and pack mule. He saddled his horse and rode out of town before the sun came up. It was going to be a long day in the saddle; Luke wanted to make it back to the ranch before dark. He didn't want to spend another night sleeping under the stars this late in the year. It would get real cold once the sun went down. It had taken them two days on the drive over but without the herd to slow them down they could move faster and cover more ground and they should make it back in one day. He alternated his pace between a trot and a fast walk and occasionally when they came to a long flat stretch of the trail he would spur his horse into a gallop for a short distance but he knew better than to push his horse too hard.

It was getting late in the afternoon and they had left the pine forest behind as the trail wound it way through the low laying sage brush and canyons close to home. They should make it back to the ranch before dark. Everything was going good and Luke could relax and enjoy the quiet scenery around him the rest of the way home.

Luke was soaking in the beauty of the familiar countryside when he thought he saw a movement part way up the side of the canyon just ahead. He pulled his horse to a stop to get a better look and sure enough there it was again but what was it. Then it slowly came into focus, a beautiful mule deer buck feeding on the side of the ridge. Luke sat there on his horse studying the situation for a minute. The buck was too far away to get a good shot at from here but maybe if he left the horse and mule here he could work his way up a small gully to his right and then come up out of the gully and when he got to the top of the ridge between the gully and the deer he should be close enough to get a shot at it. He would be down wind from the deer all the way and if he was quiet the deer shouldn't spook or take off before he could get off a shot.

Luke dismounted and took off his spurs and hung them on the saddle horn, they would make too much noise when he was walking and scare the deer for sure. He tied his horse to a bush then he pulled his 30 30 out of the scabbard, levered a shell into the chamber and started his stalk. He worked his way up the gully until he figured he was about even with the deer and then snuck up to the top of the ridge and peeked over the top. He was in luck; the buck had actually moved down the ridge a little ways and was feeding right in front of him about fifty yards away. He took careful aim just behind the front shoulder and squeezed the trigger. The 30 30 barked once and the buck humped his back, staggered a couple of steps and collapsed in a heap. The shot had gone right through his lungs. Luke gutted the buck and dragged it down the side of the ridge to the trail and went back to get his horse and the pack mule. He loaded the deer on the pack mule and continued his trip home.

The sun went down and it was starting to get dark and they still had a ways to go before they got back to the ranch. But luck was with them because a full moon was just starting to come up over the Bradshaw Mountains behind them and it gave them enough light so they could easily see and follow the trail. They would be home shortly.

They rode into the ranch yard under a full moon that was now high enough in the sky to light up the yard like it was the middle of the day. Luke dropped the deer off by the wood shed behind the house. Then he took the horse and pack mule to the barn unsaddled the horse and removed the pack from the pack mule. He gave the horse a good rub down and a bucket of oats and got them settled for the night and then headed for the house. He dragged the deer into the wood shed and hung it up. He would skin it and cut it up tomorrow. It would be cold enough at night now so the meat would keep for a long time hanging in the wood shed. He cut the liver and heart out of the deer and took them in the house. He would have some liver for supper tonight and save the heart for another day. It had been a long day and it felt good to be home again.

CHAPTER THREE: Prescott

Luke shifted uncomfortably on the wagon seat as the wagon bumped along the deeply rutted road leading into Prescott. His butt was getting sore from sitting so long on the hard flat surface of the wagon seat on the long ride from his ranch. He would much rather had spent the long ride on horse back and in a saddle than on the wagon seat. The saddle was made to conform to the curvature of his butt where as the wagon seat was just a flat board with splinters in it. But he needed the wagon to haul his supplies back to the ranch so he had no choice but to bring the wagon today.

They had left the low laying sage brush and small scattering pines behind them and were now in the tall Ponderosa pine forest near Prescott which meant that it shouldn't be too much longer before they would be in Prescott. The team just kept plodding along at the same pace as if they knew where they were going and that they were in no big hurry to get there. All they had to do was follow the road and with the trees growing so close on both sides of the road there wasn't much chance of them getting off the road.

Luke wrapped the reins around the brake lever and just kind of let the horses go it on their own. He reached into his shirt pocket and pulled out his harmonica and started playing a tune on the harmonica. He was about half way through *"Turkey in the Straw"* when one of the wheels on the wagon dropped into a hole in the road and he just about fell off the wagon seat causing him to hit a couple of sour notes. One of the horses whinnied and shook her head in disapproval; she didn't like it when he played off key. On long trips like this he would change off playing the harmonica and singing songs to help pass the time away. It also seemed to have a soothing effect on the horses, as long as he didn't hit too many sour notes. He liked to sing ballads and a couple of his favorites were *"Little Joe the Wrangler" and "When the Work's All Done This Fall"* and some times he would just make up his own little ditties as he rode along depending on what kind of mood he was in like:

The old gray mare she shit on the whipple-tree*
She shit on the whipple-tree; she shit on the whipple-tree
The old gray mare she shit on the whipple-tree
Many long years ago

He would have to remember to clean off the whipple-tree when they got to Prescott.

*Foot note: a whipple-tree is that part of the wagon that the harness traces are attached to. It is about 3 feet long and 3 inches thick and is right under the horse's tail when the horse is hitched to the wagon.

There was still plenty of daylight left when they came out of the Ponderosa pine forest on to White Spar Road and turned on to Montezuma Street going down past Whiskey Row and the Courthouse Square headed for the OK corral and livery stable down by the railroad station. Luke parked the wagon beside the livery stable and unhitched the team. He led them over to the watering trough and let them have a good long drink of water before he took them inside where the stable boy Billy, some people called him the kid, helped him take off their harnesses and get them settled in their stalls. He made sure they had plenty of hay and were settled for the night before he went back out to the wagon and cleaned off the whipple-tree. Then he headed for the hotel and restaurant.

Luke checked into the hotel and went up to his room to clean up before he went down to the restaurant for his supper. After supper he sat around the hotel lobby for awhile visiting with a couple of the other ranchers before he went back up to his room and turned in for the night. He thought about heading over to Whiskey Row for a drink before he called it a day but it had been a long day and he was tired, maybe tomorrow he would feel more like spending some time in the bars.

The next morning Luke slept late then got up and had a leisurely breakfast. After breakfast he moseyed over to the Courthouse Square. He visited a little bit with Sheriff Bucky O'Neill then sat around for awhile waiting for the bank to open. When the bank finally opened he went in and cashed the bank draft he had received when he sold his herd in Crown King. Then he headed down to the livery stable to pick up his horses and the wagon. Billy helped him harness the horses and get them hitched to the wagon then he started out to do his shopping.

His first stop was the lumber yard/hardware store. He needed some lumber, barb wire, and some kerosene for his lamps and lanterns. He had better get some more nails and staples. He also needed some blocks of salt for the cattle and a new set of hinges and a latch for the outhouse door. He was going to have to fix the outhouse door to keep the snow out this winter. It was bad enough sitting down on that cold seat in the winter time without having to brush the snow off the seat before you sat down. He got everything loaded in the wagon and double checked his list to make sure he had everything he needed. When he was satisfied that he had everything he climbed aboard the wagon and moved on.

His next stop was Babbitt's Mercantile, he gave Bruce Babbitt his grocery list, oatmeal, coffee, flour, sugar, salt, baking power, a tub of lard, tobacco, a 50lb bag of navy beans, a 50lb bag of pinto beans, *"beans beans the musical fruit the more you eat the more you toot, the more you toot the better you feel so lets eat beans for every meal,"* two 50lb bags of potatoes, some can peaches, can pork and beans, and some can vegetables. While Bruce was filling his order he looked around the store to see if he could find anything else he might want or need. He picked up a new deck of cards, some dime westerners to read and he came across a coupled of books by someone name Zane Grey; THE HASH KNIFE OUTFIT and ARIZONA AMES. He had never heard of Zane Grey but they looked like they would be good reading and with the long winter months coming up he decided he would get them and add them to his small library. Bruce had his grocery list filled now. He double checked the list with Bruce then paid him for his purchases and loaded them in the wagon. He hoped that he had enough to see him through the winter. Then he climbed onto the wagon and headed back to the livery stable.

Luke parked the wagon beside the livery stable and unhitched the horses and led them over to the watering trough to get a drink of water before he took them back into the barn to take off their harnesses and put them back in their stalls. Then he went back to the wagon and covered everything with a tarp. He secured the tarp making sure to tie down the corners real good so no wild animals could crawl up under the tarp and get to his groceries. When he was satisfied that he had everything secured and that it would be safe for the night he went to get some lunch

After he finished his lunch he headed over to the Goldwater Department Store. Barry Goldwater greeted him with a handshake when he walked in the door, always the politician, and asked him if he could be of any help. The first thing on his list was a new pair of boots and some socks. He picked out six pair of socks and put one pair on before he started trying on the new boots. Luke tried on four or five pair of boots before he found a pair that was comfortable and fit just right. He asked Barry if they could please put his old boots in the box, he wanted to wear the new boots when he left the store. Next on his list was a pair of heavy duty leather gloves, a couple pair of Levis, 34X32, and three flannel shirts, medium. He liked the ones with the checker board square design rather the ones with the stripes. He didn't care what color they were. With winter coming on he needed a couple of pair of long johns, heavy flannel underwear, the only color they had was red but that was all right as long as they would keep him warm this winter. That should about do it, he said. Barry wrapped up his purchases and tossed in a couple of big red bandanna handkerchiefs as token of appreciation for his business. Luke paid Barry his bill and gathered up his purchases and headed back to his hotel room.

Once he was back in his hotel room he unwrapped his purchases and laid them on the bed then he picked out a new shirt, a new pair of Levis and a new pair of long johns. He rolled them up and stuck them under his arm and headed over to the barbershop. He got a shave and a haircut and then spent the next half hour bathing and soaking in the barbershop bath tub. Then he got dressed in his new set of clothes. He felt like a new person now that he was all cleaned up and dressed up in a new set of clothes. It was getting close to supper time so he took his old clothes back up to his room and headed down to the restaurant for supper.

After supper Luke headed over to Whiskey Row for a couple of drinks and to see what was going on. He sat in on a poker game for a few hands but the cards were not falling his way tonight so he folded his hand and left. He had a drink with one of the ladies and went up to her boudoir with her for awhile then headed back to his hotel room.

The next morning Luke got up early and after breakfast he checked out of the hotel and headed down to the OK corral and livery stable. He put the packages with his clothes in them under the wagon seat. Then he checked the tarp covering his purchases of yesterday to make sure everything was still secure. When he was satisfied that everything was all right he went into the stable to get his team. Billy helped him harness the team and hitch them to the wagon. He paid Billy his livery stable bill and wishing the kid good luck he climbed on to the wagon seat. Picking up the reins he released the brake on the wagon and slapped the horses on the rear with the reins and said giddy up. The team leaned into their collars and as the slack in the harness traces tightened up the wagon slowly started to move forward. They had come into town pulling an empty wagon now they were headed home with a fully loaded wagon. A much heavier load than what they had come in with. The only good thing was that it was mostly down hill all the way back to the ranch. Luke waved good-by to Billy as the team pulled out of the livery stable yard and started down Montezuma Street past Whisky Row and the Courthouse Square on the way out of town. The place was deserted this early in the morning. The only one Luke saw was a drunk sleeping it off on the courthouse steps. Some of these young cowboys just couldn't hold their liquor.

The road wound its way through the tall Ponderosa Pines and straightened out a little bit as it dropped down into the smaller pine forest and the low laying stage brush. They turned off the main road just before they got to Wilhoit crossing over a small ridge and dropping down into the valley where the headwaters of the Hassayampa River were formed. That road followed along the banks of the Hassayampa River all the way back to the ranch.

When they reached the Hassayampa River Luke let the horses pause for a drink of water.
Then he pulled the wagon over under a large cottonwood tree so they could rest for awhile.
His butt was getting sore from the long ride and he had to get down off the seat and walk around a little bit to stretch his legs. He had the cook at the restaurant fix him a couple of egg and baloney sandwiches this morning while he was eating breakfast so he ate the sandwiches now washing them down with a drink of water from his canteen. They were making good time and should be back at the ranch well before dark. After a short rest Luke climbed back up

on the wagon seat and they continued their journey home. Things were kind of quiet so Luke started singing:

*A group of jolly cowboys discussing friends at ease
Said one I'll tell you something, boys, if you will listen please
I am an old cowpuncher, boys, and here I'm dressed in rags I use to be a good one, boys, and go on great big jags*

*I used to have a home, boys, a good one you all know although I haven't seen it, since long long ago
When I left my home, boys, my mother how she cried,
For me her heart was broken, for me she would have died*

*I am going back to Dixie once more to see them all
I am going to see my mother when the works all done this fall
That very night the cowboy went out to stand his guard.
The night was dark and cloudy and storming very hard*

*The cattle they got frightened and rushed in wild stampede.
While the cowboy tried to head them, while riding at full speed
While riding through the darkness so loudly did he shout. Trying hard to head them and turn the herd about*

*His saddle horse did stumble and upon him it did fall
Now he won't see his mother when the works all done this fall
They picked him up so gently and laid him on his bed
His body was so mangled the boys all thought him dead*

*But he opened up his blue eyes and looking all around
He motioned for his comrades to set near him on the ground
And when the boys were seated all around his bed
He opened up his pale lips and this is what he said*

Joe you may have my saddle, Jim you may have my bed
George you may have my pistol after I am dead
Send my wages to my mother the wages I have earned
And tell her I won't see her although my heart does yearn

They buried him at sunrise no tombstone at his head
Just a little slab and this is what it said
Poor Charlie died at daybreak his saddle horse did fall
Now he won't see his mother when the works all done this fall

Luke loved that song even though it made him feel sad every time he sang it. Poor Charlie, what a way to go, but that is the life of a cowboy, you have to take your chances never knowing what will happen next. It was getting late and they were getting close to home. As they passed through the River Pasture a couple miles north of the ranch. Luke noticed a cloud buildup over to the southwest. It was that time of the year when the storms could pop up unexpected at any time. He was glad this one held off until he made it back from Prescott and he wondered whether this one would bring some rain or some snow or both. It could start out as rain early in the evening and as the night got colder it could turn in to snow. If they got some thunder and lighting with it which did happen once in awhile then the locals would call it thunder snow.

The sky was getting darker and the cloud build up was getting closer when they pulled into the yard at the ranch, but still no rain. They had made it home before the rain started. Luke pulled the wagon up beside the ranch house and unloaded the groceries and took them in the house before he drove out to the barn. He pulled the wagon into the barn and unhitched the team. He would unload the rest of the wagon tomorrow. Luke put the team in their stalls and took off their harnesses. He gave them some hay and got them settled for the night. Then he went over to the corral to check on his saddle horse before he headed for the ranch house. The saddle horse still had hay in the feeder and water in the drinking trough so he would be all right for tonight.

It had been a long trip but a good one and Luke was glad to have it over with. He had made it to Prescott and back before the winter storms set in and he had gotten the supplies that he needed to see him through the long winter months that were just ahead. He had reason to feel good about the way things were going right now and he started whistling a little tune as he made his way to the ranch house.

CHAPTER FOUR: Winter at the Ranch

The clap of thunder woke Luke from a sound sleep; through the bed room window he could see streaks of lighting flash across the sky as he lay there in his bed. That last clap of thunder sounded like it hit pretty close to home. He could hear the wind blowing through the trees outside and the rain coming down hard on the roof. It was November and the first winter storm of the season had arrived with a vengeance. Luke wondered if it would be just rain or if it would turn to snow before morning. It wasn't cold enough for snow when he went to bed last night but the last couple of mornings had been pretty nippy and if the temperature dropped enough tonight it could bring snow with this storm. He would find out in the morning when he got up, right now he just wanted to get some more sleep. He buried his head under the pillow and pulled the blankets up over his head, that would shut out the light from the lightning flashes and muffle the sound of the rain, the wind and the thunder so maybe he could go back to sleep.

Luke got up early after a restless nights sleep; he looked out the window at a sea of white. Sure enough it had gotten cold enough during the night to turn that rain into snow. The first thunder snow storm of the season. There would be more you could bet on that. Luke got dressed and fixed his breakfast. After he finished eating he headed for the outhouse. The outhouse door was ajar and he had to push the door aside to get in and had to brush the snow off the seat before he dropped his pants and sat down. He was going to have to fix that dang door.

It hadn't snowed a lot; there was a little over an inch or so on the level, maybe two inches at the very most. It wouldn't last long this time of the year, once the sun came out it would melt pretty fast. Most of it would be gone by the time the sun went down and by tomorrow night it would be all gone. Luke headed for the barn and got his saddle horse and threw the saddle on him. Luke climbed in to the saddle and headed for the pasture to check on the herd. He had been gone for three days and wanted to make sure they were all right. There shouldn't be any problem but with the storm last night you never knew and it is better to be safe than sorry. Luke rode slowly around the pasture checking the fence as he did so. Everything seemed to be all right and the herd was doing just fine. They didn't pay much attention to Luke because they were busy pawing the snow away trying to get to the grass under the snow. Later on in the winter when they got a heavier snow storm and the snow was deeper Luke would have to haul a load of hay out to the pasture to feed them but not today, they would be just fine. Luke rode over to the windmill and checked the water in the watering trough, there was a thin coat of ice on it but it should melt soon and if it didn't the cows could break it with their snout when they came to get a drink. It wasn't that thick so Luke just left it alone.

Satisfied that everything was all right here Luke headed back to the barn

Back at the barn Luke unsaddled his horse and turned him loose in the corral then he went to work unloading the wagon. Stacking the blocks of salt he had purchased for the cows in one corner of the barn and the barb wire in another corner. He unloaded the lumber and stacked it neatly against one wall. The nails and the staples and the new hinges and latch for the outhouse door he took to the workshop Picking up the two five gallon cans of kerosene, one in each hand, he headed for the wood shed behind the house. Passing the outhouse on the way Luke noticed the outhouse door hanging at an awkward angle on one hinge and he said to himself "I am going to have to fix that dang door." "But not today" It was a nice sunny day and the storm from last night had passed and Luke said "who needs a door on the outhouse on such a sunny day." He put the cans of kerosene on a stand in the corner of the wood shed and went into the house to fix some lunch.

As winter closed in on him Luke kept busy around the ranch making small repairs on the barn and the corral. And of course he finely got around to fixing the outhouse door. He took the door down and had to replace one of the boards in the door with some of the new lumber he had purchased. He replaced the hinges and the latch and re-hung the door making sure it fit nice and snug so no snow could get in. About every other day he would saddle his horse and take a ride around the pasture to check on the herd and make sure the fence was all right and that the windmill was working properly and pumping water into the watering trough for the herd. Late November and early December they got a couple of snow storms, not a lot of snow but the weather was colder now and the snow stayed on the ground longer and didn't melt as fast as it did in the earlier storm. A few times when he checked on the windmill he had to break the ice in the watering trough so the cattle could get some water. But so far it had been a pretty mild winter and the cattle had plenty of feed.

Just before Christmas they had a big snow storm, it snowed for two days straight, they had some thunder and lighting with it and the wind blew constantly causing some deep drifts in some places. It looked like they were going to have a white Christmas for sure, this snow was going to stay around for awhile. As soon as the storm passed Luke loaded the wagon with hay, he harnessed the team and hitched them to the wagon and took the load of hay out to the pasture for the cattle. The snow was too deep now for them to paw their way down to the grass under the snow. This time the cattle were glad to see him and they crowded around the wagon waiting for him to pitch the hay off the wagon on to the ground. The herd looked like they had weathered the storm all right. They didn't seem any the worse for wear after the storm. They all looked healthy, just hungry was all. After unloading the wagon Luke headed back to the barn. He would have to take another load out to them in a couple of days and probably some more later on, depending on how long this snow stayed on the ground. He put the team away and headed for the house, making a quick stop at the outhouse. There was no snow on the seat this time.

A few days later Luke got up in the morning and checked the calendar, unless he had missed a day somewhere along the line tomorrow would be Christmas. He should do something special for Christmas but what would he do? He was going to have to think about it. After breakfast he headed for the barn, he was going to have to take another load of hay out to the cattle in the pasture, some of the snow had melted but it was still too deep for the cattle to paw through and get to the grass under the snow. After he got back from feeding the cattle as he was walking through the barn he noticed the chickens scurrying around in the barn scratching for food and they gave him an idea. Why not make some eggnog for Christmas? There were plenty of eggs lying around the barn, more than he could eat and he had one of the cows in the barn that he was milking so he had plenty of milk. Yes that is what he would do.

Luke went around the barn and picked up a half dozen eggs from the different nests and put them in his hat to carry back to the house. Back at the house he broke the eggs and put them in a large bowl and got out the egg beater and beat them up good, and then he added the sugar, the milk, the vanilla and a touch of nutmeg and mixed it all together. He was ready to pour it into a two quart bottle when he remembered that he had a bottle of rum somewhere that he kept for medical purpose maybe he should add a shot of it to his eggnog since it was a special occasion. He found the rum and added a shot to his mix then poured it all in a two quart bottle and set it out on the porch to chill. He would enjoy it all later. Now what else should he do? He can't hang his stocking by the fireplace because he doesn't have a fireplace and Santa Claus wouldn't be able to find this place anyway, way out here in the boondocks. Pumpkin pie use to always be a part of the Christmas dinner but he didn't have any pumpkin. But he did have some squash so why not make a squash pie. It was not as good as pumpkin but it would be all right. He got a couple of squash and cut them up and made his filling. Then he got the flour and lard and made his pie crust and put it all together in a pie pan and put it in the oven, it will take about an hour to bake.

While the pie was baking Luke headed back out to the barn. That old rooster had been on a mean streak lately picking a fight with the younger rooster and it even went after him the other day. He didn't need two roosters with his small flock of chickens so if he could catch him he would roast him for his Christmas dinner. Luke chased the rooster around the barn for awhile, finely catching him by throwing a horse blanket over him. Picking him up by the legs Luke carried him squawking and flapping to the woodshed. Picking up the ax in one hand he laid the roosters head on the chopping block and with one quick blow it was done.

Luke tossed the carcass into the snow where it flopped around spraying blood all over the landscape, turning the white snow red. While the rooster was flopping around in the snow, saying his last goodbyes Luke went back in the house and got a bucket of hot water from the boiler on the kitchen stove. Taking the bucket back out to the woodshed he picked up the rooster and dunked it in the bucket of hot water and then he started picking off feathers tossing them on the ground where the wind picked them up and scattered them around the yard. He had to dunk the carcass in the bucket of hot water a few times as he finished picking it clean of feathers. Then he gutted it, cleaned it all up and hung it on the porch to air. It would be all right there tonight and he would put it in the oven tomorrow it should only take three or four hours to roast it before dinner. Then Luke got the pie out of the oven and set it on the table to cool. The eggnog had been cooling on the porch for a few hours now and should be ready to drink so he poured himself a glass and sat down to drink it. It tasted pretty good. He was proud of himself that he had remembered how to make it.

Christmas morning Luke got up and had his breakfast then he went out to the barn to do his chores. He had taken a load of hay out to the cattle in the pasture yesterday so they would be all right, he wouldn't have to check on them today. After he finished his chores he went back to the house and started fixing his Christmas dinner. The first thing to do was to get that old rooster in the oven because it was going to take the longest to cook. He made some stuffing with some bread crumbs and some spices and stuffed it inside the rooster and put the rooster in the oven. It would take three or four hours to cook and he could just sit back and take it easy for awhile. Luke got out his bible and read both Matthew's story and Luke's story of the birth of Christ, He liked Luke's version better that he did Matthew's version. He could relate better to the shepherds than he could to the wise men Then he just puttered around the kitchen getting things ready for dinner.

Before he sat down at the table Luke stood there looking everything over to make sure he had everything. It looked like a feast fit for a cowboy, roasted chicken, mashed potatoes and gravy, stuffing, beans, corn, fresh baked biscuits, squash pie and eggnog. Yep he had everything he needed and he would have enough leftovers to last him a week. He sat down and said his prayer and started eating his Christmas dinner.

After Christmas things were kind of slow around the ranch. New Years came and went with no big flurry. January and February slowly passed by. Luke still had his chores to do around the ranch, he had to ride out to the pasture to check on the herd every two or three days, and take them a load of hay when the snow got too deep, but he had a lot more free time on his hands. He spent some time reading. He read the two books by Zane Grey that he had purchased when he was in Prescott, THE HASH KNIFE OUTFIT and ARIZONA AMES. He read them twice. That Zane Grey was a pretty good writer. Luke wondered if he wrote any more books, if not he should. He reread some of the other books in his small library. He had read them all before but liked to reread them all when time permitted. One of his favorites was *Two Years Before The Mast*, those sailors lived a hard life and he didn't envy them a bit. He was glad he was able to keep his two feet on solid ground and he would go crazy cooped up in such small quarters for days, weeks, and months at a time. He needed the wide open spaces that only a life on the ranch could offer.

Luke had purchased a new deck of cards when he was in Prescott so he also spent time playing solitaire. Luke also had more time now to devote to his second love, music. He would spend hours picking on his banjo and singing his favorite songs or playing his harmonica. Anything to help past the long winter days and to keep himself busy. February was slowly coming to a close and it looked like winter was about over and Luke could look forward to some warmer days ahead. He had survived another winter at the ranch.

CHAPTER FIVE: Springtime in the Mountains

When Luke got up in the morning the wind was blowing strong and there was a mixture of snow and rain falling from the sky and it was cold outside. If the old saying was true that when March comes in like a lion it will go out like a lamb then the end of March should be sunny and warm. It was the first day of March which meant that spring would be just around the corner. The weather in March could be so unpredictable it could be nice and sunny and warm one day and cold and rainy the next day with a slight chance of snow just when you would least expect it. And the March winds blew all the time, cold from the north and warm from the south and the ever changing east and west winds. The winds from the east coming down off the Bradshaw Mountains were usually cold after they crossed over the snow covered peaks, where as the westerly winds coming up from the desert were usually a little warmer. Luke would have to adjust his work schedule now to conform to what the weather would allow but it meant he would be spending more time working outside. But there wasn't much he could do today until the snow and rain stopped.

The next morning when Luke got up the snow and rain had stopped so it was time to go to work. His first job was to clean the manure out of the corral and get rid of the pile of manure behind the barn that had accumulated during the winter. Luke hitched the horses to the wagon and started shoveling. He cleaned out the corral first hauling the manure out to the hay field and spreading it around to help fertilize the hay field. It was hard work pitching the manure around the field by hand and Luke wished he could afford one of those new manure spreaders that he heard a guy named McCormick had invented. You just hooked it to the back of the wagon and shoveled the manure into it and it threw the manure all over the place. They said that it would spread the manure a lot more even than you could by pitching it by hand. Maybe some day he would get one, he would have to put it on his wish list. It took Luke a week to get the manure all cleaned out of the corral and the pile behind the barn hauled away.

It was calving time for the cows so Luke had to keep a close eye on the herd to make sure that there were no problems. One day when he went to check on the herd he found a dead calf, he had no idea what happened to it but he had noticed that it had never looked real healthy. Luke threw a rope around it and dragged it over to the edge of the pasture with the mother cow following along behind mooing loudly. Luke untied the calf and threw the rope around the cow's neck and led her to the barn. He would use her for a milk cow since the cow he had been milking had gone dry and he had turned her loose in the pasture with the rest of the herd. Then he got a shovel and rode back out to where he had left the calf. He dug a shallow grave and buried the calf. If it had some type of disease he didn't want it spreading to the rest of the herd.

Luke had a small area that he had used for a garden last year so he spent some time digging it up and working up the soil so it would be ready for planting. He would plant some sweet corn, tomatoes, squash and some other vegetables when the time was right but it was too early to do any planting yet.

March had suddenly come to a close. It was now the first week in April. The calving period was over with and there had been no major problems, the weather was warming up and now it was time to start thinking about the spring roundup and branding. He could use a little help with the branding but first he would have to lend a hand to one of his neighboring ranchers. Luke saddled up his horse and tied his bedroll behind the saddle and rode over to John Hays ranch in Peeples Valley. John had a much bigger ranch than Luke and had a few full time cowboys working for him. When Luke got there they had already started their roundup. Luke put his gear in the bunkhouse and rode out to the pasture where they were working.

John Hays was glad to see him; he said they could always use an extra hand during the spring roundup and branding. Luke spent a week there working, eating and sleeping in the bunkhouse with John's crew. It was hard work but Luke enjoyed every minute of it. It was nice to have someone else to talk to besides himself and his horse. When the branding was over with and the herd returned to the range, Luke got ready to head back to his ranch. John Hays gave him a year old colt that had never been ridden and sent one of his top wranglers with Luke to help him with his roundup and branding. The wrangler's name was Juan and he spoke very little English but he knew his way around horses and cattle and Luke was appreciative of his help. Luke and Juan rode back to his ranch leading the new unbroken colt. The colt was frisky and didn't want to be led so they had their hand full getting him back to the ranch. It was late in the afternoon before they got back to the ranch; they put the colt in the corral and rode out to the pasture to check on Luke's herd before they unsaddled their horses and turned them loose in the corral. They would start the roundup tomorrow.

Juan sat around on the porch relaxing while Luke went to work fixing a supper of beans, potatoes and steak. After they had eaten Juan helped him do the dishes and then the two of them played some cribbage and talked about what they were going to have to do tomorrow. They were both ready to turn in early knowing that they had a busy day ahead of them when they got up in the morning and they were both tired after their long ride today from Peeples Valley.

They were up early the next morning and after a hardy breakfast of pancakes, eggs and hash browns, washed down with a couple of cups of cowboy coffee, they were ready to go to work. They roped the colt and put him in the barn so he would be out of the way while they were working in the corral doing the branding. A frisky colt in a corral full of cattle could cause havoc and Luke didn't want to take any chances. He knew they would have their hands full as it was. Then they saddled up and rode out to the pasture where they cut out the cows and their calves and drove them into the corral. They left the bull and the steers and a couple of the cows that didn't have any calves in the pasture, they didn't need them and they would just be in the way if they were in the corral. Luke built a small fire and put the branding irons in them to heat. As soon as the branding irons were hot Juan roped one of the calves and dragged it over to the fire where Luke threw it on its side and applied the hot branding iron.

The branding was under way.

The rest of the day went on in about the same manner, Juan would do the roping and Luke would do the branding. Luke also castrated all the bull calves tossing the cutting into a bucket. He would clean them up when they got done with the branding and they would have Rocky Mountain Oysters for supper, a real delicacy. They took a short break for lunch, eating a couple of sandwiches that Luke had fixed the night before, and finished the branding by the middle of the afternoon. Juan drove the herd back out to the pasture while Luke was busy cleaning up around the corral. Once the branding fire had been put out and the hot ashes removed from the corral Luke turned the young colt loose in the corral. Luke stood there watching as the frisky colt ran around the corral kicking up his heals. He was going to make a fine cutting horse. He had spirit. Then Luke went to work cleaning up the cutting from the bull calves and started preparing his famous Rocky Mountain Oysters recipe.

They had an early supper, and then they sat around and played cards and talked until it was time to go to bed. The next day was an off day for them, they didn't get up too early and did a few chores around the house and barn and just took it easy. Luke was learning Spanish; he was getting so he understood it pretty good now and could speak it a little bit. So with Juan as his teacher Luke spent the day trying to improve on his Spanish. Juan had some good laughs as Luke would get his tongue tangled up trying to pronounce some of the words but by the end of the day his Spanish had improved considerably. You wouldn't say he was fluent in Spanish but now he could speak it well enough to get by. Juan's English had also improved so it was a day of learning for both of them.

After breakfast the next morning they saddled up and rode out to check on the herd. Luke especially wanted to check on the castrated calves to make sure they were healing all right. Everything seemed to be all right so they drove the herd out of the pasture and headed north up along the raging Hassayampa River, which was running full now due to the snow melt higher up in the mountains. They even encountered a few places where the Hassayampa River had overflowed its banks and flooded the low flat land beside the river. When they got to the River Pasture they left the herd there to graze, they would be free now to roam the open range for the rest of the summer and Luke would round them up again in the fall.

When they got back to the ranch Juan gathered up his gear and said adios and rode off to return to the Hays Ranch in Peeples Valley. Luke was sorry to see him leave, it had been nice having someone else around to talk to for a couple of days.

The cold weather was gone for this spring so it was time to plant his garden. Luke spent most of the next two days working in the garden. He hauled a small load of manure from the barn and corral and spread it around the garden working it into the soil with a shovel and rake then he planted some sweet corn, tomatoes, radishes, turnips, string beans, lettuce, onions and some squash. He would have fresh vegetables later on in the summer.

CHAPTER SIX: Summer at the Ranch

Now that the spring roundup was over, the branding was done and the herd turned loose to graze for the summer Luke turned his attention to some of the work to be done around the ranch. There were repairs to be made to the corral and the barn, some fencing to be built but most importantly he was going to have to break and train the new colt he had received from John Hays.

There was two ways to break a horse that had never been ridden before. One way was to show him who was boss, to do that you put a saddle on him, climb on to the saddle and let him buck and kick while you hung on for dear life until he wore himself out and conceded the victory to you. The problem with that way was that you would probably get thrown off a few times and could get bashed up against the corral fence a couple of times and come away so sore that you could hardly walk. Nor knowing for sure who had won the battle. Luke had seen better riders than him ending up in a heap in the corner of the corral sometimes with broken bones. The thought of that did not appeal to him and that was not the way he would go about breaking this colt.

The second way and the way that Luke was going to go about it was to win the horses trust.

That would take much longer, as long as two or three weeks or maybe even longer in some extreme cases. The first day Luke went into the corral and threw a rope around the colt's neck and wrapped the other end of the rope around the hitching post in the center of the corral. Hand over hand he walked slowly up the rope to the colt talking softly to him all the while. The colt shied away from him at first but he was finally able to get close enough to reach out and touch him. Luke patted the colt's nose then gently started patting his head and rubbing his neck, all the time talking to him in a nice quiet voice. He could feel the colt quiver as Luke ran one hand over his chest and down his forelimbs. When the quivering stopped Luke figured that was enough for today and he removed the rope from the colt's neck and let him go. The colt kicked up his heels and trotted over to the other side of the corral. Luke left him and went to work doing some repair work around the ranch.

Luke continued the same routine for a few days, spending some time each morning with the colt before he started his other work around the ranch. Luke would continue talking to the colt and some times he would sing softly as he rubbed his hands over the colt's head and neck.

Little Joe the wrangler, he'll wrangle never more
His wrangling days for ever now are o'er
He has left his spurs and saddle for the others here below

As we bid farewell to little wrangler Joe

Or one of the other many songs that he knew.

Then one morning when he opened the corral gate and stepped into the corral the colt came trotting over to him and nuzzled him with his nose, knocking his hat off his head and unto the ground. Luke laughed as he bent over to pick up his hat and put it back on his head. A bond had been formed, it appeared that the trust he needed had been established, so now he could move forward with the next phase of his training. Luke put a halter on the colt and snapped a lead rope into the ring on the halter; he would no longer need to lasso the colt and tie him to the hitching post in the center of the corral. Luke ran his hands over the colt's neck, chest and forelimbs before picking up the lead rope and started to lead the colt around the corral at a brisk trot for a short time. Luke would leave the halter on the colt so he could get use to having something on his face and head. A couple of days later they moved to the next step which was to put a bridle on the colt, he didn't like it when Luke put the bit in his mouth and he tried to chew it up and spit it out. You might say he was chopping at the bit. It took a couple of days for the colt to get used to the bridle and the bit but once he did it was time to move forward.

Now it was getting close to the time for the grand finale, the colt had never had a saddle on his back so one step at a time. Luke just put a saddle blanket on his back first and led him around the corral a couple of times, he didn't seem to mind that so next came the saddle. When Luke put the saddle on him Luke could feel him tense up and he looked back at Luke questioningly as if to ask, "What is going on?" Luke didn't tighten the clinch too tight since he wasn't going to ride him today and he just wanted him to get used to the saddle on his back. Luke led him around the corral a few times then he took the saddle off. Luke repeated this procedure for a few days until the colt adjusted to the saddle and didn't tense up when Luke saddled him.

Today was going to be the big day. It was time for the grand finale. It had been about two weeks now since Luke started breaking the colt and Luke felt it was time to climb into the saddle. Had he done a good job with his training? Would the colt start bucking? If he started bucking would Luke be able to stay in the saddle or would he end up in a heap in the corner of the corral? Luke couldn't worry about those things now; he would just have to go on about his business. Luke walked into the corral with the bridle in his hand and the colt trotted over to greet him. Luke put the bridle on him and led him over to where the saddle was hanging on the fence. Luke put the blanket and saddle on him and tightened up the clinch as tight as he could get it. He didn't want the saddle slipping around while he was in it. Holding the reins in his left hand Luke reached up and grabbed the saddle horn then he put his left foot in the stirrup and teetered up and down a couple of times trying to judge how the colt would react when he swung into the saddle. Satisfied that things would be all right he swung his right leg up and over and dropped his right foot into the other stirrup. The colt quivered and arched his back but he didn't buck. Luke leaned forward and patted his neck and whispered in his ear.

Yankee Doodle went to town riding on a pony
He stuck a feather in his hat and called it macaroni

Luke rode the colt around the corral a couple of times. It appeared that the training had gone just the way that Luke had hoped it would. Luke rode over to the gate and reached down and unhooked the strap that was holding the gate shut, he pushed the gate open and they rode out into the pasture. Luke loosened the reins and urged the colt forward. The colt responded and they raced across the pasture and back at top speed both enjoying the freedom they experienced from living in the wide open space of the high mountains. They returned to the corral, and Luke unsaddled the colt and gave him a rub down before turning him loose.

The first part of the training was done. The colt had been broken and now you could ride him. But just being able to ride him didn't mean very much, you had to turn him into a working horse if he was going to be much good to you. Next would come the task of training him to be a good cutting horse, that would be a much longer process. You would have to teach him to stand still and not move when he was ground tied. Ground tied was when you just dropped the reins to the ground and left the horse standing alone. Then you would have to teach him to respond to your body movements. A good cutting horse would stop, go, turn and cut without any command from you just by the way you turned in the saddle or applied a little pressure with your knees or legs to his side. When you were roping cattle you had your hands full with the rope and couldn't be bothered with trying to steer the horse with the reins or by giving voice commands. But the colt was young and appeared to be very smart. He hadn't learned any bad habits yet so he should be a fast learner. Luke would start the next phase of his training in a couple of days; right now he just wanted the colt to enjoy being a riding horse.

Luke was running low on supplies so it was time to make a quick trip into Prescott. He didn't need a lot so he wouldn't take the wagon this time, he would just take the pack mule and make the trip on horseback. Luke saddled his riding horse and rode out to the pasture where the pack mule had been free to roam since the spring roundup. He roped the pack mule and led him back to the corral so he would be handy the next day when Luke got ready to go. The next morning Luke spent some time with the colt, saddled him and rode him around the corral a few times. The colt was going to miss him while he was gone but he should be back by tomorrow afternoon. Then he saddled up his old riding horse and leading the pack mule he

set off for Prescott. There was a light rain coming down and Luke hoped that it wouldn't turn into a heavy downpour. He had a couple of washes to cross between the ranch and Prescott and if it started raining real hard they could be flooded. He put on his poncho and rode on.
O it ain't going to rain no more no more
It ain't going to rain no more
How in the heck can I wash my neck?
If it ain't going to rain no more

It had quit raining by the time Luke reached Prescott. The washes he had to cross had water running in them but it wasn't very deep or very swift so he had no trouble crossing them.

It was the middle of the afternoon when Luke rode down Montezuma Street past Whiskey Row to the OK Corral and Livery stable at the end of the street. He left his horse and the pack mule with Billy at the livery stable and headed for the barber shop for a hair cut and a bath. When he was finished there he stopped by the hotel to get a room and since he hadn't had any lunch today he headed for the restaurant to get an early supper. As he was about to enter the restaurant he heard some one say "Excuse me sir, could you spare a nickel for a cup of coffee?" He turned expecting to see one of the drunks that hung out on Whiskey Row, who would spent his donation on liquor rather than coffee. But there was something different about this man. His eyes were clear; he didn't look like he had been drinking. His clothes were tattered and torn but clean. He was old and walked with a noticeable limp; there was just something different about him. Luke studied the old man's face; he looked like he could use a good meal besides a cup of coffee. Luke wasn't sure what made him do it but he found himself saying "how about me buying you supper instead?" The old man's eyes lit up and he replied "OK, are you sure you want to do that?" "Yes" Luke said, "I am sure."

They went into the restaurant and took a seat at a table in one corner of the room, the waitress came and brought them each a cup of coffee and took their orders. The old man said that his name was James but everyone called him Jesse. He was from Missouri and had done something back there that upset some people and he left the state just ahead of a lynch mob. He had arrived in Prescott a couple of weeks ago and had been trying to find work but none of the ranchers were hiring and those that were wanted younger men. He had to admit that his age and his bum leg slowed him down a bit. He probably couldn't out run a rattlesnake now with his bum leg but he could still ride and rope and shoot if the need be. The waitress brought them their meals and they continued their discussion while they ate. Jesse said that if he didn't find work soon he may have to sell his horse. "You have your own horse?" Luke asked. "Yes." Jesse replied "His name is Trigger and he is a good one." Luke started thinking he hadn't come up with a name for the colt yet; he had better start thinking about that. Also he had to hire someone part time to help him with some of the work around the ranch, and he was going to need some extra help with the haying this summer. His herd was getting bigger so maybe it was time to hire someone full time. Maybe that was the reason for their chance encounter today. So he said to Jesse. "If you want a job, I have one for you. I can't pay much, fifteen dollars a month and keep for you and your horse is about all I can offer, but if you are interested the job is yours." Jesse just about choked on the piece of steak he was eating. He looked at Luke in disbelief, "do you mean it?" he said "I'll take the job. I am sure it beats robbing trains."

As they were leaving the restaurant Luke told Jesse to meet him in front of the Courthouse Square on the west side of the Courthouse about 9:00 o'clock tomorrow morning and they would ride back to the ranch together. As they started to part Jesse turned to Luke and said, "I know we just met and you don't know much about me yet but could you advance me five dollars on my salary? I would like to get a new pair of Levis and a new shirt before we leave town." Luke gave him the five dollars and watched as Jesse hurried off towards Goldwater's Department Store before it closed for the day. The old man seemed to have a new spring in his step. Luke wasn't sure why but he seemed to trust the old man, Jesse, James or what ever his name was it really didn't matter.

Luke turned and headed over to the Bird Cage Saloon on Whiskey Row. He got himself a drink and sat in on one of the poker games going on at one of the tables. Lady Luck was with him tonight and he won a few dollars before he cashed in and went looking for Jan B. He found her and spent a pleasant evening with her in her boudoir before heading back to his hotel room.

After breakfast the next morning Luke went down to the OK Livery stable and got his horse and pack mule, he paid Billy for their keep and rode over to Babbitt's Mercantile. He had to increase his order on some items since he would be having another mouth to feed now that he had hired Jesse to work for him. He gave Bruce his order and while Bruce was filling his order he looked around the store. He found a couple of more books by Zane Grey, *Sunset Pass* and *The Dude Ranger* so he got them to add to his library. After Bruce got his order filled he paid Bruce and Bruce helped him carry his order out and load it on the pack mule. Once everything was secured on the pack mule, he rode over to the Courthouse Square to meet Jesse.

Jesse was waiting for him, all spruced up with a new shirt and a new pair of Levis. Luke sat on his horse and watched as Jesse limped over to his horse, a beautiful strong looking palomino with a long flowing white mane. If nothing else that old man sure knew about horse flesh. That horse would bring top dollar in just about any sale, hands down. Luke couldn't remember of ever seeming a better looking horse in all his life. Jesse climbed into the saddle and the two of them rode out of town heading back to the ranch.

Back at the ranch the first thing Luke did was to go and check on the colt. "Did you miss me boy?" Luke asked. The colt nodded his head as if to say yes. Luke rubbed his head and neck and then went to unloaded his supplies. Luke and Jesse unsaddled their horses and turned them lose in the corral and turned the pack mule loose in the pasture, they wouldn't have any need of the pack mule for awhile. Then they went into the ranch house and put away their supplies and sat down to discuss what Jesse's duties would be. On their ride back from Prescott, Jesse had said that he could cook but he had to admit that he wasn't a real good cook. But Luke was willing to take a chance on his cooking, so his first job would be to take over the cooking and the household duties. That would give Luke more free time to spend training the colt to be a cutting horse and doing the heavy work around the ranch. If Luke needed help with anything Jesse would be expected to give him a hand. But his main job would be the cooking and cleaning for now and some chores around the barn, milking the cow, cleaning out the barn and taking care of the garden.

Jesse accepted his duties with enthusiasm; he went right to work and fixed supper for them that night. It was nothing fancy but Luke had to admit that in may have been a tad better than his own cooking. That gave Luke a chance to spend some time with the colt that evening. He saddled him and rode him around the corral for awhile, he was responding well to Luke's commands and Luke decided on a name for him he would call him Champ, because he was going to be a champion cutting horse when Luke got done training him. Things were looking good, it was going to be a busy summer, they still had the haying to do and some fences to build but now Luke knew he would have some help when he needed it.

When the alfalfa was ready for the first cutting, Luke harnessed the team and hooked them to the mowing machine and went to work. He mowed the alfalfa one day and let it dry out for a couple of days before he got out the dump rake and raked it into piles. Now he was going to need Jesse's help hauling the hay to the barn. The next few days Luke and Jesse worked side by side in the hay field pitching the hay unto the wagon, hauling it to the barn and then pitching it off the wagon into the haymow in the barn. It was hard work and Luke wondered if Jesse would be up to the task but Jesse held his own. Maybe he didn't move as fast as Luke and sometimes he would have to stop and rest for a bit but he did a good job and Luke was glad he was there to help. They filled the haymow in the barn to the rafter and started to build a haystack in the corned of the pasture. There would be a second cutting of the alfalfa later on that summer and they would add that to the haystack when the time came. They should have plenty of hay for the herd this winter when the snow came.

Luke didn't have much time to spend with Champ, the colt, while they were doing the haying but now that the hay was taken care of he could get back to his training. He and Jesse took it easy for a couple of days. Luke spent more time working with Champ while Jesse took some time to just relax and rest. Then Luke decided it was time to ride out and check on the herd so one morning he and Jesse both saddled up and they rode up to the River Pasture, that is where they would start the search for the scattered herd which could be anywhere this time of the year. They spent the day riding up and down the side canyons around the River Pasture and up to the top of Fire Clay Hill and back, finding a few cows and steers scattered here and there. They didn't see any sign of his bull anywhere but all the cattle they saw were in good shape and Luke figured the old bull must be hiding out some where and he would be all right. Once Luke was satisfied that they were all ok they rode back to the ranch. They would make two or three more trips to checks on them later on in the summer. They would probably find the old bull on one of those trips.

Luke continued working with Champ, his training was coming along real good and Luke figured that by the time it came time for the fall roundup he should be ready to do the work of a cutting horse. Luke wanted to fence in the hay field so he could use it for pasture in the winter time, the herd was getting to large for the pastures space he had now. He could have done it all by himself but Jesse gave him a hand and the two worked side by side digging post holes, setting the post and stringing the barb wire. It was much easier with two of them, especially when it came to stringing the barb wire, which was hard for one man to do by himself.

The last part of July and the first part of August brought the monsoon rains which caused the Hassayampa River to start running full again. It also brought much needed rain to the alfalfa and the pasture. Luke and Jesse made another trip up to the River Pasture to check on the herd, most of the herd was feeding in the River Pasture this time which was now covered in a thick layer of green grass brought on by the monsoon rains. The bull was with the rest of the herd this time, not off by himself like he was the last time they checked. Satisfied that most of the herd was there and in good shape they didn't spend any time checking the side canyons or ride up to the top of Fire Clay Hill. They just circled around the pasture and rode back to the ranch.

The monsoon rains were over with in late August but Luke waited until early September to give the alfalfa field time to dry out before he started the second cutting of the alfalfa. This time it went a little faster because they were adding the alfalfa to the haystack in the corner of the pasture rather that putting it into the barn. It was much easier to just pitch it off the wagon on to the haystack than it was to pitch it into the haymow in the barn. But it was still hard work and old Jesse did his share without grumbling.

Now that the haying was done and the fence had been built it was time to take it easy for awhile and start thinking about the fall roundup. But there was one more thing Luke wanted to do before the fall roundup. He wanted to ride over to Crown King and talk to the owner of the mine to see how many steers they would want to buy this year. The last couple of years they had purchased his whole herd between twelve and eighteen steers but this year he was going to have over twenty five to sell and he wasn't sure if they would take all of them and he didn't want to drive them all over to Crown King and have to bring some of them back home again. It would also be a good test of how well his training had gone with Champ because he would be riding Champ off the ranch for the first time.

Luke saddled up Champ one morning and started off for Crown King. Champ seemed to enjoy the change of scenery and responded well to Luke's commands. They arrived at Crown King late in the afternoon and Luke left Champ at the livery stable and went directly over to the mine's office. He sat down with the mine's owner and they had a drink together while they discussed business. The owner said that the maximum they could take would be eighteen of the steers. They just didn't have the facilities to handle any more than that at one time. He would prefer to take just fifteen this year. They would wait until the herd was delivered before they would agree on a price. He wanted to wait and see what kind of shape the herd was in before he would talk money. They were satisfied with the beef that Luke had delivered in the past and were sure this herd would be in as good of shape as the others had been. They closed the deal with a hand shake and Luke headed over to the hotel to get a room and some supper.

After supper Luke spent the evening with Big Bertha before he went up to his room and turned in for the night. The next morning he picked up Champ at the livery stable and they started their trip back to the ranch arriving home late in the afternoon. It had been a good trip. He had accomplished what he had set out to do and had given Champ his first real test as a working saddle horse, which he passed with flying colors.

That evening after supper Luke and Jesse started making plans for the fall roundup, which would begin in less than a month. This year would be different than in years past, Jesse would be there to give him a hand and for the first time he would have some help with the fall roundup. It would bring to a close another summer at the ranch high on the western slopes of the Bradshaw Mountains.

About the Author

George Davison is a retired accountant who has turned to writing in his retirement. He was originally from Michigan and got shipped out to California by the Navy, fell in love with his wife, Mary, settled in Arizona, and had a couple kids. This is his second book. He has written many poems to great accolades of his readers including a poem about the Granite Mountain Hot Shot crew who lost their lives in 2013 defending the town of Yarnell where George has a home.